DANTDM (REAL NAME DAN MIDDLETON) IS ONE OF THE WORLD'S TOP YOUTUBERS. DAN STARTED MAKING VIDEOS WHILE HE WAS A STUDENT AT THE UNIVERSITY OF NORTHAMPTON. SOON AFTER, IN 2012, HIS CURRENT MINECRAFT-FOCUSED CHANNEL WAS BORN—*THE DIAMOND MINECART // DANTDM*. HE NOW HAS FANS ALL AROUND THE GLOBE AND MAKES VIDEOS THAT ARE WATCHED BY MILLIONS OF PEOPLE EVERY DAY.

DAN LIVES IN THE UK WITH HIS WIFE, JEMMA, (ALSO KNOWN AS *XXJEMMAXX*) AND THEIR TWO PUGS, ELLIE AND DARCIE. THIS IS HIS FIRST BOOK.

THIS BOOK IS FOR MY WIFE, JEMMA.

MY PUGS. EVERY SINGLE MEMBER OF TEAMTDM.

AND EVERY MEMBER OF MY FAMILY THAT

SUPPORTS ME; YOU KNOW WHO YOU ARE.

TRAYAURUS AND THE ENCHANTED CRYSTAL

DanTDM

ILLUSTRATED BY
DOREEN MULRYAN AND MIKE LOVE

HARPER
An Imprint of HarperCollinsPublishers

ISBN 978-0-06-257432-9 (TRADE BDG.)—ISBN 978-0-06-267653-5 (SPECIAL EDITION)

18 19 20 LSCC 10 9
❖
FIRST AMERICAN EDITION
ORIGINALLY PUBLISHED IN GREAT BRITAIN IN 2016 BY TRAPEZE,
AN IMPRINT OF THE ORION PUBLISHING GROUP LTD.
THIS EDITION INTENDED FOR THE SCHOOL MARKET ONLY.

TRAYAURUS AND THE ENCHANTED CRYSTAL

HEY THERE, EVERYONE—DAN HERE AND WELCOME TO MY BOOK! THANK YOU SO MUCH FOR CHOOSING TO BUY MY FIRST EVER GRAPHIC NOVEL. IT'S BEEN A VERY SPECIAL PROJECT, AND I'M SO GLAD YOU'VE DECIDED TO TAKE THIS JOURNEY WITH ME.

YOU MIGHT KNOW ME FROM MY VIDEOS, ESPECIALLY MESSING AROUND WITH MY FAVORITE MINECRAFT CHARACTERS LIKE TRAYAURUS, GRIM, CRAIG, AND MANY OTHERS. I LOVE CREATING STORIES AND ADVENTURES FOR THEM ONLINE SO MUCH THAT I WANTED TO TAKE THEIR STORY FURTHER IN A MEGA-QUEST—AND THAT'S RIGHT HERE IN THE FOLLOWING PAGES. WITH NO LIMITS TO THE KIND OF ESCAPADES WE COULD GET UP TO IN THIS BOOK, WE DELVE HEADFIRST INTO AN EPIC ADVENTURE, A STRUGGLE FOR POWER, AND WE MAKE BOTH FRIENDS AND ENEMIES ALONG THE WAY.

I DECIDED TO WRITE THIS BOOK FOR THE SAME REASONS I STARTED DOING YOUTUBE VIDEOS— BECAUSE I LOVE BEING CREATIVE, PLAYING GAMES, INVENTING STORIES AND HAVING FUN IN THE PROCESS. WHEN I FIRST BEGAN MAKING VIDEOS, HARDLY ANYONE VIEWED THEM, BUT NOW I HAVE ONE OF THE MOST-WATCHED CHANNELS IN THE WORLD—AND IT'S ALL DOWN TO YOU GUYS! YOU HAVE ALL BEEN A HUGE SUPPORT; WATCHING, LIKING, AND INTERACTING WITH MY VIDEOS EVERY SINGLE DAY, MAKING ALL OF THE HARD WORK WORTHWHILE. I HOPE THIS PROVES THAT IF YOU KEEP DOING SOMETHING WITH PASSION, WORK HARD, AND NEVER GIVE UP, YOU'LL EVENTUALLY HAVE OPPORTUNITIES TO DO BRILLIANT THINGS.

THIS GRAPHIC NOVEL IS ONE OF THOSE THINGS. THE IDEA CAME ABOUT BECAUSE I WANTED TO CREATE SOMETHING NEW FOR ALL OF US TO ENJOY, AND THIS HAS DEFINITELY BEEN ONE OF THE MOST EXCITING THINGS I'VE WORKED ON. FROM PLOTTING THE STORY, EVOLVING MY CHARACTERS, ADJUSTING THE COLORS, PLANNING THE BACKGROUNDS, AND LAYING IT ALL OUT, THIS BOOK HAS SURE BEEN A WHIRLWIND COMPARED TO MAKING VIDEOS! I HAVE LOVED BEING ABLE TO TELL A STORY VISUALLY, AND HAVING THE CHANCE TO WORK WITH AMAZING ARTISTS HAS BEEN A BLAST. I AM A HUGE GRAPHIC NOVEL FAN, AND I HOPE THAT BY READING THIS, YOU WILL BE TOO (IF YOU'RE NOT ALREADY).

SO HERE GOES. THIS IS MY WORLD OF IMAGINATION ON A PAGE—YOU CAN NOW SIT DOWN WITH A STORY STRAIGHT OUTTA MY BRAINBOX! HOPEFULLY YOU WILL ENJOY IT AND IT WILL INSPIRE YOU TO KEEP BEING CREATIVE, FOLLOWING YOUR DREAMS, AND MAKING STUFF—JUST LIKE DAN AND TRAYAURUS IN THEIR LAB.

OK, INTRODUCTION OVER. LET'S DO THIS!

DanᗢTDM

TRAYAURUS

DR. TRAYAURUS (OR JUST TRAYAURUS FOR SHORT) IS A
BUDDING SCIENTIST WITH HIS VERY OWN LAB. FROM A
YOUNG AGE, TRAYAURUS STARTED MIXING LIQUIDS, COMBINING
MATERIALS, AND STUDYING ANYTHING HE COULD TO FULFILL HIS
PASSION FOR SCIENCE. UNFORTUNATELY FOR HIM, HE WAS BORN
WITH EXTREME CLUMSINESS, A CONDITION THAT CAUSES HIM
TO MAKE LITTLE MISTAKES IN HIS AMBITIOUS EXPERIMENTS
WITH DISASTROUS RESULTS. HOWEVER, WITH HELP FROM HIS
BEST FRIEND, DAN, THINGS ALWAYS WORK OUT IN THE END, NO
MATTER HOW BIG THE MESS.

DAN

DAN IS A HAPPY,
ENTHUSIASTIC, AND FUN-
LOVING INDIVIDUAL.
A LOVER OF ADVENTURE
AND PURSUER OF ALL
THINGS EXTRAORDINARY. DAN AIDS
TRAYAURUS WITH HIS EXPERIMENTS
DAY IN, DAY OUT, INTENT ON EXPLORING
ALL THINGS WEIRD. DAN MET TRAYAURUS AFTER
MOVING NEXT DOOR TO HIS LAB AND HAS NEVER
LOOKED BACK, DESPITE A SLIGHT DISAGREEMENT
ABOUT A GIANT PET DRAGON THAT TRAYAURUS
ONCE OWNED. DAN ALSO OWNS A VERY
SPECIAL DOG CALLED GRIM, WHO WAS
ONCE A PERFECTLY HEALTHY, REGULAR
DOG, BUT ONE UNFORTUNATE EXPERIMENT
LATER, GRIM IS NOW A LIVING SKELETON
VERSION OF HIMSELF. THEY HAVE BEEN
INSEPARABLE EVER SINCE.

DENTON

NO ONE IS SURE WHERE DENTON CAME FROM OR WHY HE IS SO UPSET WITH EVERYONE HE MEETS. HE RUNS HIS OWN LAB, WHERE HE CONDUCTS EVIL EXPERIMENTS TO AID HIS ULTIMATE PLAN OF WORLD DOMINATION. AT HIS COMMAND IS A GROUP OF ELVES, ALL OF WHOM WERE EMPLOYED BY HIM AFTER HE BUILT OVER THEIR SETTLEMENT WITH HIS GIANT LABORATORY. WITH THEIR LEADER, FIN, AS DENTON'S RIGHT-HAND MAN, THE ELVES NOW AID DENTON IN HIS EVIL PLANS. DAN, TRAYAURUS, AND DENTON HAVE CROSSED PATHS IN THE PAST, WITH DENTON BEING BEATEN EACH TIME, LEAVING HIM WITH A STRONG DISLIKE TOWARD DAN AND TRAYAURUS AND SEEKING REVENGE!

FIN

BEING THE LARGEST IN SIZE, FIN WAS THE NATURAL LEADER OF THE ELF COMMUNITY. BUT WHEN DENTON BUILT HIS LAB OVER THEIR SETTLEMENT, IT THREATENED THEIR VERY EXISTENCE. NATURALLY PERSUASIVE, FIN USED HIS CHARMS TO ENCOURAGE DENTON TO TAKE HIM AND THE ELVES ON AS LAB ASSISTANTS SO THEY WOULDN'T BE LEFT HOMELESS. DENTON RECOGNIZED FIN'S QUICK THINKING AND EFFICIENCY AND EMPLOYED HIM AS HIS SECOND-IN-COMMAND. EVER SINCE, FIN HAS STOOD LOYALLY BY DENTON'S SIDE, LEADING MANY OF HIS EXPERIMENTS.

PIGS

THE PIGS WERE YOUR NORMAL, EVERYDAY PIGS UNTIL ONE OF THE YOUNGER FEMALES WAS BESTOWED WITH THE POWER OF SPEECH. IT TURNS OUT THAT SHE IS VERY GRUMPY MOST OF THE TIME, THOUGH SHE HARBORS A SECRET SOFT SPOT FOR DAN AND TRAYAURUS. BUT DON'T YOU GO TELLING THEM THAT!

WH-WH-
WHAT?!

THE
CLONING
MACHINE...
IT WORKS!

WHUMP

GRIM!

I'M SORRY, BUDDY—LET'S GO AND SEE TRAYAURUS!

TRAYAURUS OFFICE

TRAYAURUS... *TRAYAURUS!*

WHAT IS HE *UP* TO?! HE'S USUALLY UP FIRST.

TRAYAURUS?! WE'RE COMING IN...

3....

2....

1...

...HERE I COME!

WAG WAG

LET'S BEGIN!

FLIK

FLICK

ENTER

BOOF

SHHUNK

WE'RE COMING DOWN!

TAKE THAT CRYSTAL TO THE CLONING ROOM. WE'VE GOT TO TEST IT *IMMEDIATELY!*

YES, SIR!

WHAT ARE WE GOING TO DO?

CREATE MORE CLONES, BUT WITH *DOUBLE* THE POWER!

THEN WHAT ARE WE WAITING FOR?! LET'S GO!

HEY, *I'M* THE BOSS HERE. I SAY *"LET'S GO."*

PULL A LITTLE HARDER!

W-WE'RE TRYING!

KEEP GOING!

WHOA!

WOOSH

CLUNK

HAHAHAHAHA! I'LL KEEP HOLD OF THIS ONE MYSELF!

HOW DID YOU *FIND* US?

YOU HEAR THAT *NOISE?*

THAT *BEEPING SOUND* LED US STRAIGHT TO YOU. WHAT IS IT, ANYWAY?

BEEP

BEEP

I'M NOT TELLING YOU.

OOOOHHH... AAGGGHHH!

EXCELLENT! YOU FOUND IT! GOOD WORK!

AND NOW THE *FINAL PIECE* OF THE PUZZLE...

HAND IT OVER.

HAHA HAHA!

DING

MEET TEAM DANTDM...

DANTDM

WROTE THE STORY LINE, CREATED THE
CHARACTERS, AND OVERSAW THE WHOLE
BOOK THAT YOU'RE READING TODAY!

MIKE MARTS

IS THE PERSON WHO BROKE DOWN DAN'S
SCRIPT AND CREATED THE COOL, FAST-PACED
NARRATIVE TO ACCOMPANY THE PICTURES.

CORY PETIT

IS THE MASTERMIND BEHIND THE
AWESOME VISUAL SOUND EFFECTS,
LETTERING, AND SPEECH BUBBLES.

DOREEN MULRYAN

IS THE WONDERFULLY CREATIVE ARTIST
WHO SET THE STYLE FOR THE STORY AND
TRANSFORMED DAN'S WORDS INTO PICTURES.

MIKE LOVE

IS THE EXTREMELY TALENTED
SUPPORT ARTIST WHO HELPED BRING
THE WORLD OF DANTDM TO LIFE.

JULYAN BAYES

IS THE DESIGNER WHO HELPED TO
ADD THAT ALL-IMPORTANT SPARKLE
TO THE REST OF THE BOOK.

A SPECIAL THANK-YOU TO
EMMA KUBERT, LISA FOWLER LUBERA, MARKI WOLFSON, JARED OSBORN,
AND DAVID FORREST AND HIS TEAM AT KINETIC UNDERGROUND.